CW01574869

FIRST STORY

First Story's vision is a society that encourages and supports young people from all backgrounds to practise creative writing for pleasure, self-expression and agency. We believe everyone has a unique voice, a story to tell and a right to be heard. Our flagship programme places inspiring professional writers into secondary schools, where they work intensively with students and teachers to develop young people's creativity, confidence and ability. Through our core provision and extended opportunities, including competitions and events, participants develop skills to thrive in education and beyond.

Find out more at firststory.org.uk

First published 2023 by First Story Limited
44 Webber St, South Bank, London SE1 8QW

www.firststory.org.uk

ISBN 978-0-85748-582-3

1 3 5 7 9 10 8 6 4 2

A CIP catalogue record for this book is available from the British Library.

Printed and bound in the UK by Aquatint
Typeset by Katie McLean
Copy-edited by Kirsten Irving
Proofread by Sarah Donnelly
Cover designed by Jenny Dack (overtdesign.co.uk)

Trying To Do A Pull-Up With Your T-Rex Arms

An Anthology by the First Story Group
at Titus Salt School

Edited by Andy Craven-Griffiths | 2023

FIRST STORY

Contents

Introduction

Andy Craven-Griffiths, Writer-in-Residence

Another lovely First Story project at Titus Salt School, and as usual, it's been my favourite teaching work of the year. The group have been brilliant, and I want to mention a few of my own personal highlights. The group poems were a strong start to the project and the group grasped incredibly quickly the power of good creative writing craft. I love the specific detail in lines like, 'Crying while watching sad Bollywood movies with your Mum.'; the showing-not-telling in lines like, 'Seeing a police officer eating a doughnut.'; the humour in, 'Insulting someone in a different language when it turns out they know that language.', and the use of personal voice and vocabulary in, 'Getting an elite new haircut and people making fun of it, even though they're bald.'

This year, I introduced the idea of writing with only two rules: 1) The writer must believe what they are writing (within the world of the poem or story); 2) The writer must be engaged in some way by the piece they are writing.

Again, these young writers learnt quickly. When I felt someone had written something for speed or convenience, I asked them whether they believed it. They usually agreed they didn't, and willingly improved it. When they did believe it, they argued for it and usually I was convinced. Aamna's story about Miss Vickery, for example, takes a sudden weird and magical turn, and I believe it. I believe the human reactions and choices, which is what we need to believe – not that the story could happen in our world, but that we believe the emotions and choices of the characters in the imagined world.

We spent an entire session on beginning from *telling* emotions and situations, then working in small teams to convert them into *showing* emotions and situations. This seemed to pay dividends once we were editing first drafts of stories, and the improvements were huge and immediate. In Eleanor's story 'The Executioner' (which has the brilliant set-up of an executioner who no longer wants to kill), 'He was sick of it' became, 'The executioner was sick of the cracking sound of the spine as the axe went through their necks.'

It is always wonderful to see attitudes change – or at least soften – towards writing. I am thinking particularly of Paris, Estelle and Neve, all of whom missed some sessions and were sometimes a little reluctant. All three wrote strong pieces. Paris poured out some brilliant work in the last week or two of the programme. Estelle got a special mention in the national Six Word Story Competition, and the showing-not-telling in her 'Mother Time' story is superb. Neve got a special mention for her story 'Goldfish' in the national 100 Word Story Competition and that was a first draft! I hope all three have proven to themselves that the idea they might not like writing, and might not be good at it, is not necessarily true.

I want to mention the resilience of the group as well: those who did multiple edits on stories really got to see the benefits. I'm thinking of Emily's story 'Telemachus Wants a Suit', Hector's 'The Briefcase' and Jemimah in everything she wrote – especially the final two lines of 'Jess on the Train', written in collaboration with Emily, which show maturity in not *telling* the reader what to think or feel, but instead showing an image and allowing us to think and feel what we will, based on that image. We also tried writing dialogue in a new way: simply writing two characters (A and B) talking to each other, then editing to add conflict, and to have each character to try to get what they want, rather than simply answering the other. I hope you enjoy Jemimah and Kinza's dialogues here.

There are lovely lines and details throughout. Dexter has a talent for peppering his work with fun details relevant to the story: Froppy the Frog's local news being Ferret News, her car being a Koi-ota and his phone being an iFrog 10x are all indications that Dexter might enjoy leaning into the world-building of fantasy writing. Leia's use of the senses and concrete detail when describing Courage as smelling, 'like the forest: grass, bugs, pond, mud' and feeding, 'off its surroundings, eating bark, berries and leaves.' Joseph's story idea of the owl who wants to swim is brilliant, as is Isaac's story 'Action!', with its clever reveal.

As always, I thank everyone at Titus Salt for making this project so successful: Francesca Skaife, for her tireless support and extra efforts in running the cover-and-title session after the workshop weeks were over (on top of everything else). Kate Metcalfe, for giving the students her help and writing expertise. Liz Chillington, for filling in when we needed somebody to cover, and for being a big part of why First Story even happens at Titus Salt. Thank you to the art team for their illustration workshops, and to the student artists for their illustrations, which always add an extra layer to the anthologies. Finally, I give huge thanks to our student ambassadors, Sam and Milly, who ran exercises, shared great examples (especially in the dialogue writing) and were generally a positive influence throughout.

Enjoy *Trying To Do A Pull-Up With Your T-Rex Arms*!

Teacher's Foreword

Francesca Skaife (Leader of English Transition) and Kate Metcalfe (Literacy Co-ordinator)

Creathinkers (creative + thinkers)
= the definition of our lovely bunch of writers this year.

What a year it has been! What a write it has been! We are into our seventh year with First Story at Titus Salt School and the talent, commitment and creativity of our pupils has continued to bamboozle and beguile us. Steered by resident writer's Andy Craven-Griffiths' steady hand, our writers have collaborated to a wonderful collection of poetry and short stories over the sixteen sessions of the programme.

It hasn't been without its problems. We've dodged strike days, hurdled snow days and side-stepped sickness to emerge, blinking, into the glorious light of a finished anthology. It's funny, it's thought provoking, it's heart-wrenching, it's unfathomably weird in places… and it wouldn't have happened without the concerted efforts of the dedicated people who propelled it across the finish line.

Firstly, thank you to the incomparable Andy Craven-Griffiths, who took our rough little diamonds and polished them to a shine worthy of a Rihanna song. The pupils have loved the games and the fun, but more importantly, they have learned bucketloads from his tips, tricks and lessons on the editing process.

Secondly, we would like to thank our First Story support team, including Claire Sharples, our interim Regional Programme Manager, who supported us in getting the programme started this year and helped us launch last year's book too, and our new Regional Programme Manager, Ali

Johnson, who joined us for fun and frivolity on World Book Day. Thanks also to Sophie Blacksell Jones for keeping us on track through the production stage, Jenny Dack for designing our wonderful front cover and Kirsten Irving for answering all of our last-minute emails in record time, and for having such a great sense of humour. We look forward to many more years of collaboration with them.

Thirdly, to our incredibly talented artists Jen Dewhirst and Chloe Chatburn for running an illustration workshop again this year. With their guidance and expertise, the pupils have perfectly captured the imagery created by our writers and we couldn't imagine the anthology without them now. Our collaboration with the art department was particularly pertinent this year, as our World Book Day theme was 'The Power of Graphic Novels'. The combined power of text and sketch, word and shape, story and scape brings meaning to life and we hope you enjoy the pairings in this anthology. To our Year Nine illustrators, we were in total admiration of the standard you produced in only two hours. We wish you all the best on your GCSE Art journey, and it's an A* from us.

Thanks also to Tom White Jennings for his technical expertise in filming our writing sessions; our efforts live on in multimedia form, and it's very exciting!

Penultimately, thank you to our lovely admin team and our unrivalled leaders, headteacher Mr Morrel and English Faculty Leader Liz Chillington. We continue to count our blessings for being able to continue our partnership with First Story and to Mr Morrel for giving us his support to change the lives of our writing cohorts every year.

Finally, of course, thank you to our fabulous writers! They have proved again and again that their creativity holds no bounds. Our wonderful crew of Year Eight and Year Nine writers

– and not forgetting our sixth-form ambassadors, Milly and Sam – have lived and breathed their creations, nurturing a great word here and the odd line there into beautiful blooms of poetry and stories. This final product is testament to their dogged determination to make something to be proud of, and proud we are. Not only have they learnt the potency of their own wordcraft, but they have also grown to know themselves and their minds much better. It has been a privilege to watch this journey and they can all look forward to bright futures.

BUS
STOP
BUS

All These Terrible Things

Various Authors

Earrings that don't go through your ear.
When you fail at something.
When you wake up to your alarm at 2 a.m.
Being helped by someone who hates you.
Slow walkers.
When you try really hard on your sports team and your team calls you useless.
Coffee cake.
Doing your homework last minute, then it doesn't go through, so you get detention.
The smell of bad milk.
Getting an elite new haircut and people making fun of it, even though they're bald.
Ravioli.
Global warming.
Playing a game that disconnects when it's almost finished.
Boring dreams.
Running for the bus and missing it as everyone watches.
Rotten eggs.
Insulting someone in a different language, when it turns out they know that language.
Driving while it's dark.
When you get locked outside after break.
Soggy socks.
When you're in goal and the ball bends back your fingers.
Dropping a stitch while knitting and not noticing until it's too late to fix.
Tomato puree.

DRIVING WHILE IT'S DARK.

Drinking orange juice after brushing your teeth.
Blocked noses.
When your girlfriend / boyfriend breaks up with you.
Your favourite team losing and people going on about it the next day.
Tripping into a puddle.
Spilling your drink on your new white top.
Trying to sing along to a song when you don't know the words.
Dog lips.
Feeling tired and proud that you've walked a long way, then remembering you have to walk back the same distance.
People chewing with their mouths open.
Someone stepping on your shoe.
Pineapple on pizza.
In the bath, when the tap drips cold on your legs.
Getting sand in your sandwich.
Food that's so oily you can see the oil leaking out.
Having to play football at 9 a.m.
Thinking you know the answer and being proven wrong.
A soggy burger.
Wearing 'Tuesday' socks on a Thursday.
Nails on a chalkboard.
Your laptop going *ping* to notify you it is about to die.
Socks with holes in.
New pants that are uncomfortable.
Blocks of butter.
The feel of sandpaper on your hands.
Dad's farts.
Being off school but being too sick to enjoy it.

Action!

Isaac Wilson

Running for my life, I leap on to the wing of the moving plane, right next to the propeller. With sweaty palms, I pull myself up onto the tail. I overhear air-traffic control give the pilot confirmation that the runway is clear. The roar of the engines gets louder and louder, making my body tremble and my ears feel like they're going to burst. As I climb onto the roof, the pistol in my pocket moves around and reminds me of my mission.

'CUT!'

'Thank God for that,' I mutter as I walk over to food truck at the other side of the set.

The Briefcase

Hector Sheehy

A man dressed in full black overalls snuck around the back of the Mayor's house, crawled up the drainpipe and just watched. Finally, when the clock showed five past one in the morning, he sprang into action. Silently, he slid open the window and stepped inside the building. He pulled open drawers, searching and searching. Finally, he found what he was looking for: a hidden drawer under the bed. He opened it to discover a jet-black briefcase with a gleaming silver handle. Grabbing his find, the man jumped out of the window, sliding down the drainpipe like it was a fireman's pole. He trampled through the bushes, tripping on tree roots still wet from the rain earlier that miserable autumn day. When he finally got back to his house, he took off his balaclava and soaked pants, put the briefcase under the stairs, went to his laptop and messaged his friend: 'Got it!'

The next morning at precisely ten past eight, the man declared, 'It's time!'

He opened the briefcase and examined the contents. Then he cut two wires: one red and one blue.

'It's not working!' he exclaimed.

Suddenly, the briefcase started beeping.

'Oh no!' he thought, panicking. 'It's too late!'

At once, the phone of every person across town rang in unison. The man quickly closed his laptop and ran out of the house, throwing his phone away as he went, leaving the briefcase sitting in his house. He ran through the streets of the deserted town, covering his ears to block the noise.

'I need to get out of here, I need to get of here!' he repeated.

All of a sudden, the Mayor's voice boomed out across the town:

'We know you are out there. You can run but you cannot hide!'

In the distance, the man could hear faint groans and gurgles. Of what? Hypnotised people, or something more sinister? He started running but it was too late: he was surrounded. The townsfolk started closing in, murmuring like zombies.

'Please God, help me!' the man cried. They edged closer, until he could feel and smell their breath. He closed his eyes and braced for impact, but then abruptly it fell silent. He opened his eyes to see their bodies lifeless on the ground.

'What the… ?'

Six-Word Stories

Various Authors

Poverty,
death, war,
disease – keep scrolling.

Estelle Outlaw-Bentley

Claw
marks
everywhere. Cat was out.

Paris Dosanjh

Man
in chimney
had no beard.

Isaac Woolford

Boy
loses girl.
Girl loses mind.

Jemimah Baylis

Class
is quiet,
nooses hanging outside.

Joseph Hopton

Went
to aquarium.
Boss was fishy.

Dexter Yorke

Froppy the Frog and the Lily Pad Loan

Dexter Yorke

There was once a frog called Froppy. Froppy was a fun frog but one day she wanted to move out of her parents' house and buy her very own lily pad. She reached into her raggedy trousers and pulled out a few fly-coins and a button. One lily pad cost one thousand fly-coins. Froppy went to get a loan, but once she had done that, she realised she couldn't afford to pay it back. She would need to get a job.

That's when Froppy remembered the night of the thunderstorm when she was just a small tadpole. How their old lily pad was tragically burned after a lightning strike. How her parents were interviewed by reporters on that fateful night and how, afterwards, she pretended to be a reporter interviewing her teddies on her old bed.

When Froppy went for her job interview at Ferret News, she was immediately noticed for her impressive talent for reporting and hired on the spot. It was all so fast that it felt like she had skipped a part of her life.

At first, people frowned when she asked them questions, and walked in the opposite direction. But she kept on trying and eventually got to interview famous golfer Croaker Swan-Beats. She asked how he'd got into golf and if he'd considered it as a career. He answered all of her questions and gave her a five-star review on Kelp. This caused her name to skyrocket.

When Froppy eventually gathered up enough money to pay back the loan, she discovered her loving parents had already handed over the money to the bank as a gift to her for making their lives worth living. Froppy could now buy her own Koi-ota and a brand new iFrog 10x. She visited her parents, hugged them and couldn't help but tear up.

Froppy visited her parents often and lived a happy life as a reporter. Reporting even led her to meet the love of her life, Gareth Grooch, the famous painter, teacher and soon-to-be father of two talented young tadpoles.

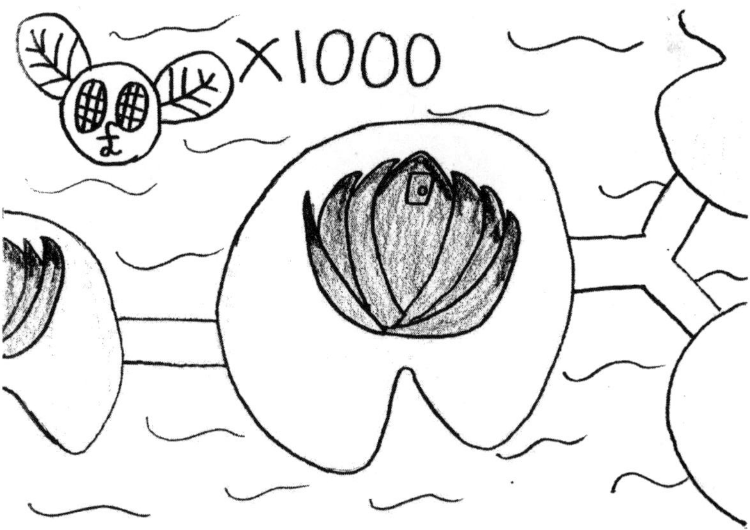

Telemachus Wants a Suit

Emily Noble and Jemimah Baylis

Telemachus the business giraffe wanted a suit from the suit shop, *Suit's Me!* It needed to fit him so he could go on tour with his giraffe band. Giraffes need special suits so their necks don't get cold. When Telemachus asked for a loan at the bank, though, they said no, as he'd asked too many times before.

Telemachus went to ask his Grandma Rita for help. She always had biscuits. He still dreamt of his suit, but he was also happy with biscuits. The next day, Telemachus went to tell his band the bad news. They said it was ok – he didn't need a suit. He was happy until he found out *why* he didn't need a suit. They were kicking him out of the band, since they couldn't get a microphone tall enough anyway and he was always taking all the attention.

Telemachus the attention-seeking business giraffe went home to his wife. She welcomed him in and gave him a cabbage to make him feel better. Gratefully, he accepted the gift and ate it while watching his favourite TV show *Giraffe Wipeout* (where they make giraffes do funny obstacle courses and fall off into the mud).

He was happy to forget his worries, just lazing around watching TV and eating his cabbage.

Telemachus the lazy, attention-seeking business giraffe woke up with a headache. He was tired from staying up all night.

He jumped out of bed as he realised this wasn't his house.

He started tiptoeing downstairs, checking if there was anyone else in this house. He didn't want to be seen or heard. Downstairs, he stepped on a wobbly floorboard. Oh no! He might get caught! He could have been heard! He heard another creak, but he hadn't moved. Who could it be?

Scared, Telemachus sprinted out of the house. As he looked back, he saw his wife staring through the window. He stumbled, tripped and fell.

'How long have I been here?' he thought. 'Who am I?'

Sitting up slowly, the now-nameless giraffe looked around. He was in a misty and unforgiving forest without an end. This was not where he had fallen!

He decided to walk around and explore his surroundings. Lots of little dots speckled the air. That wasn't a good sign. Was he starting to become unconscious again? No! Now he could *feel* the dots. They got bigger, consuming his vision. Only when they cleared could he see the flashing lights around him.

Again?

A muffled voice spoke, and Telemachus could just make out what they were saying.

'Welcome back to *Giraffe Wipeout*, where we already have a casualty!' The audience laughed while something came and picked him up, wiping him down with a sponge.

'Now, who are you, young giraffe?'

He looked up at an extremely tall giraffe staring back at him. How was this 'young giraffe' supposed to answer that when he had been asking the same exact question to himself for what seemed like a lifetime?

'I… Umm… Ermmm… I'm… Pete. Pete Peterson, Sir.'

Why would this random guy who didn't know anything about him believe a stupid name like tha –

'Everyone, please say a big welcome to our new contestant, Pete Peterson!'

Having dodged, tumbled, rolled and jumped, Pete Peterson looked back one more time at the disaster zone of broken competitors and almost felt pity. That was, until he heard the host say that he was the winner! He had never felt so happy in his life (except for the time his uncle had given him a lifetime's supply of cabbages).

Telemachus the winning, lying, lazy, attention-seeking business giraffe skipped back home.

Crispy the Crocodile

Charlie Turner

Crispy the Crocodile wanted some friends but no one wanted to be friends with him. Fortunately, he found a brave, courageous and noble hare. Unfortunately, Crispy didn't know how to feed Harry the Hare.

A week earlier, Harry had had a family, but when he was running with his brother, he got lost. Fortunately, after a day, he found his way home. During his day of being lost, his family had disappeared from his home. Fortunately, he found them outside, getting ready for school. When he got to school, he was always the smallest hare there. He was also the most timid. He always found a way through the day, but he had a bully called Big Bad Barry.

It was also his little brother Timmy's first day at that school and Harry was very scared for him. As Big Bad Barry went up to Timmy, Harry ran in front and specked Barry so they had to move away and go to another school.

It was going well until one of his friends said, 'Let's go into the sludgy swamp,' and that was the day he got lost from his home. Over those two days, he became more courageous, more brave and more noble, and that was why he wasn't afraid of Crispy. Eventually they both bumped into each other and sat down to have a little talk, to get to know each other more.

Crispy said, "Well, my story is that I once had a family and… "

A snake had slithered its way up the side of the convocation.

'Carry on,' said Slappy the Snake, his tongue shaking.

Crispy, surprised, said, 'I once had a family, and it was the best time. I loved every single second with them, but one day they all just disappeared from me. I was camouflaged from them, so they probably forgot me.'

'What's your story, Slappy?' Harry asked.

'I don't really have one,' said Slappy.

'Come on, you have to have one,' said Crispy.

'As I said, I do not have one!' shouted Slappy.

'OK, OK,' said the others, in disappointed voices.

They all fell asleep for the night. During the night, Harry felt a tickling on his back. It was a mouse. As Harry screamed, Slappy launched at him, ripping the mouse apart, and that was the night they became friends.

They started off the next day with a walk to find Harry's relatives, but as they were walking along the path, they found a llama, who came out of nowhere. In front of them all, he started crying, saying, "I lost them, I lost them." They calmed him down and asked him who he had lost.

'I lost my family. They left me,' said Larry the Llama, so they decided to find his family too. They wandered off into the field and found a village, and then eventually found a farm, but Larry's parents were not there and had moved to another farm. They went to the other farm and finally found Larry's parents, and after that they carried on with their journey to find Harry's family.

Eventually, after two days had passed, they went past

Harry's old school, which he hadn't been to in over a week. They ran into Barry again, but Barry got so scared at the sight of Crispy that he stuttered something and ran off in terror.

They then found Harry's old house and there was his brother in the driveway, sat there in despair. At the sight of Harry, his face filled with joy as he was finally reunited with his brother. Timmy realised there was a crocodile and a snake behind him and hugged his brother tighter because he was scared at the sight of them but Harry managed to calm him down so that he was confident enough to say hello to them.

After a while, they all started to play together and have a lot of fun. They used Crispy as a slide and Slappy as a swing-set on a tree. As it got to sunset, Crispy and Slappy decided to go back to the swamp and get some rest, so they said goodbye and went their separate ways and didn't see each other for a while.

The First Owl to Swim

Joseph Hopton

As the dawn broke over the valley, the morning birds woke up singing their sweet little songs. The pinky-red sunlit sky was shining on the green trees. All of the animals were waking up for the day ahead, but for one little bird it was going to be a very important day. The owl's little eyes fluttered open. He knew this would be a day of extreme training, but not to fly, like the average stereotypical owl. He was going to be the first owl ever to SWIM!

The owl hopped out of his little tree-stump home and pushed away the ivy blocking the sun, so the light partially blinded him. After his eyes had adjusted, he walked along the path with a spring in his step. He hopped up to grab a leaf from the big sentinel tree. He also collected a few berries, took a little drink from the brook and strapped on his goggles.

At the water's edge, he looked out across the lake with the lilies blooming in the sun, the reeds a light green. He tentatively put his foot into the water, then he jumped back from the cold. He knew he needed endurance to do this, and a bit of cold water couldn't stop him so early. Taking a deep breath in, he put his foot back into the water, but then he lost his balance and SPLADOOSH!

The water erupted. The little owl's head was under the water, and he started to panic. Gasping for air, he went desperately in any direction he could, until finally his head popped up above the surface. Flapping his wings, he flew to the water's edge and lay down, tired. Trying to catch his breath, he gulped and realised it was going to be hard.

For the rest of the day, he tried and tried again. By the time dusk had dawned, he knew he'd had his last practice for the day. He slumped his wings down and hung his head, and a lone tear fell onto the floor. He moved the ivy leaves and closed them behind him. He jumped on his bed and cried rivers of tears. Maybe he would not be the first owl to swim.

The next day, when the sun rose, the morning birds did not sing. The little owl flew up to the top of his tree and sat there all day, doing nothing and saying nothing.

Just then, a fox looked up into the tree and asked him why he was so sad. The little owl replied, 'I thought I was going to be the one owl in the world to swim, but now the hope has gone.'

The fox said that he had experienced the same thing when he was a young fox and had tried to become the first fox to learn to climb trees. The fox showed him and shimmied up the tree up to the owl.

'Don't fall at the first obstacle!' said the fox, jumping down the tree and disappearing.

This little comment helped the little owl's hopes and he flew up to the top of the sky and sang his song. He then flew back down to the river with a big boost of energy. This time he did slightly better but still had to gasp for air. Pulling himself out of the river, he took a few deep breaths and said to himself distinctly, 'I can do this, I can do this, I can do this.'

Ignoring his feelings and working his brain to the max, he jumped back into the river and moved his arms with some sort of symmetry. He kept himself afloat for a few minutes but then he lost his breath and sank down. As he gasped for air, he chanted his maxim to himself and kept doing the motions that had been keeping him up. When he got a bit tired, he got out of the water and stood there thinking to himself, 'That was fun.'

Then it dawned on him: he had been swimming and he hadn't even realised! He jumped for joy, then jumped back into the river and swam off into the sunset.

Seven Ways to Annoy Your Cat

Paris Dosanjh

1. Throw cat toys at it really fast so it gets excited.
2. Keep roughly tickling its stomach with a feather and grab its paws so it gets annoyed.
3. Chase it really fast around the house and jump out from corners.
4. Try grabbing its toys off it and teasing it, but make sure it doesn't claw you.
5. Give it ear scratches when it's eating and stroke its tail so it gets angry.
6. Meow back at it when it wants you to turn the tap on for it, and don't turn it on.
7. When you're going to sleep, pick it up and chuck it outside, then shut the door so it doesn't wake you up in the middle of the night.

Better Names for Animals

Various Authors

Beaver:	Bob the (dam) Builder
Cat:	Supercalifragilisticexpial-Ferocious
Chicken:	Flappy Bird
Clam:	Salty Margarita
Dog:	Sir Poopsalot
Duck:	Quacky Yellowball
Flamingo:	Pink Lollipop Stick
Fox:	Catdog
Hedgehog:	Spikerduke
Racoon:	Joseph
Seagull:	Beach Chicken
Snake:	Murder Noodle
Stingray:	Majestic Sea Flap-Flap
Swan:	Gliding White Demon
Worm:	Organic Noodle

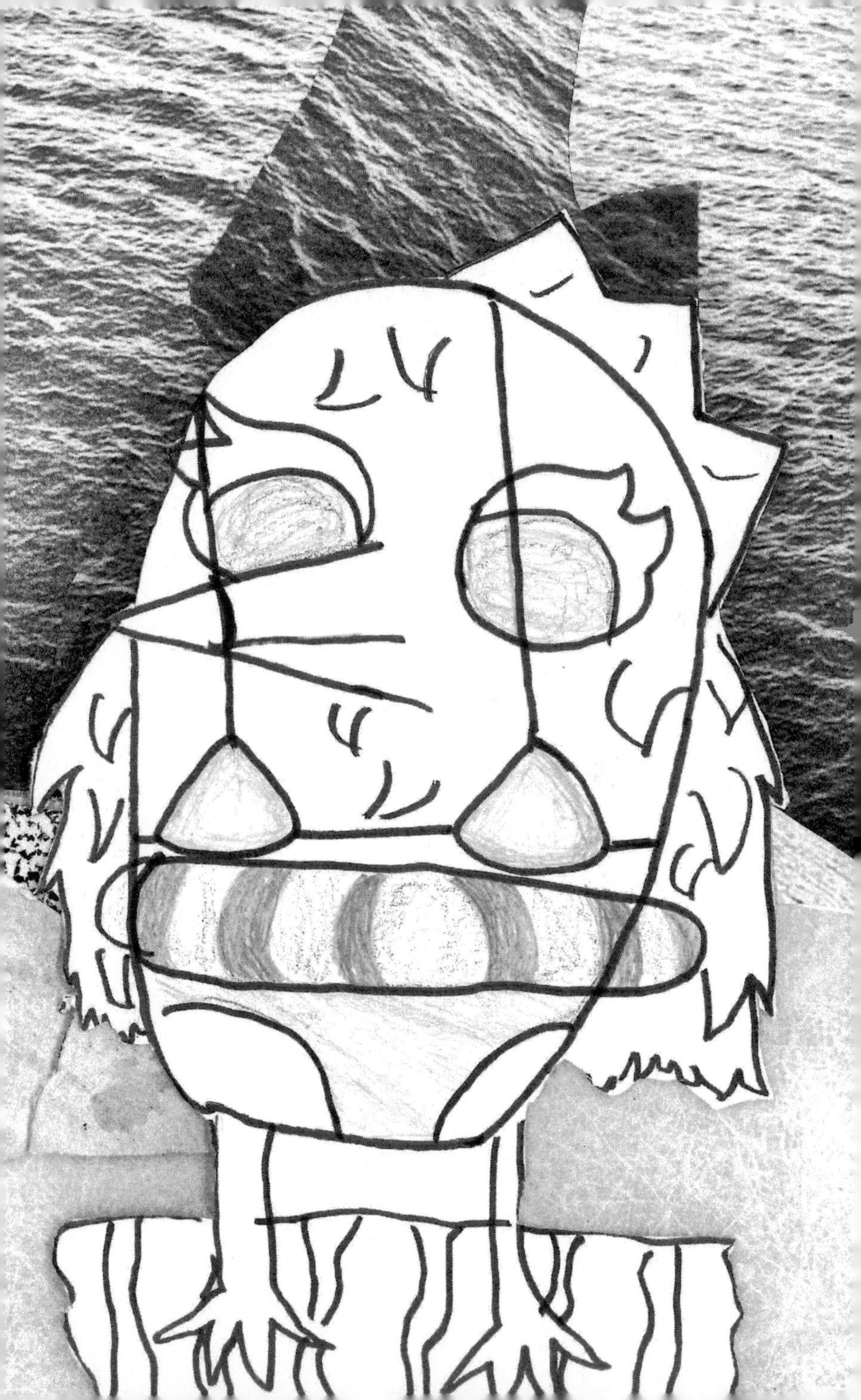

If You Wake Up as a Dinosaur

Various Authors

ROAR! Like your mum shouting at you.
Eat some people for fun, and to know what they taste like.
Learn how to poo like a dinosaur – Squat? Shake?
Stomp on buildings.
Find a pink T-Rex with a bow on its head and befriend them.
Eat. Sleep. Mate. Repeat.
Use T-Rex arms for something useful.
Realise you're extinct, so you're dead.
Play basketball with dinosaur-lovers.
Eat. Sleep. Mate. Repeat.
Try to make people understand you are really human.
Try to do a pull-up with your T-Rex arms.
Try to have a good night's rest with blankets and pillows to
warm your cold blood.
Moan because you can't find skincare for your dry scales.
Eat. Sleep. Mate. Repeat.

Miss Vickery Wants One Peaceful Day

Aamna Hussain

Miss Vickery woke up from a bad dream one morning and remembered she had to go to work. She was already regretting the day because Mondays were always bad days. Her eyes were still closed, but she had no choice but to work if she wanted to earn money.

She went to wash her face. To her surprise, the tap water was warm! With a smile on her face, she got dressed and headed to work, where the headmaster told her that her she was covering another class today. Miss Vickery looked down in despair and walked off to her classroom.

A few hours later, the time came when she had to teach the horridest class in the school, 8C4. Oddly, when the pupils walked in, they did not make a sound. Instead, every student had a petrified look on their face. Not a single word throughout the whole lesson. The thing Miss Vickery didn't know was that when she was dreaming about getting chased by a pterodactyl, her face had turned into a dinosaur's face.

At the end of the day, she skipped out of the school to her car with high hopes. Unfortunately, the car would not start. Then the other teachers came past, heading home. Fortunately, one of those teachers was her best friend. When her friend came, she shrieked in horror at Miss Vickery's horrific dinosaur face. When Miss Vickery looked in the mirror, she screamed too.

The Lucky Escape

Paris Dosanjh

Elena was trapped inside her school after a very weird event. She was in the bathroom and heard a massive bang, then the sound of something soft falling onto the floor. She stepped out of the cubicle and saw a few piles of clothes on the floor, but the students had disappeared. She ran up the stairs, back to her classroom, but all of her friends were gone with only their clothes and stationery left behind. All of the teachers just turned and walked out of the room. They looked normal, except for one difference: their eyes were red.

Elena found an empty classroom to hide in; luckily it was unlocked. She peaked out of the door but there were teachers guarding the ends of the pod; she had to think of a way to escape! She crawled into the staff room, where Ms Moon was, and hid under the table. Ms Moon had red eyes too. She also had a huge, unsettling smile, and a bag beside her, big enough to fit a few people inside.

Elena spotted a stapler on top of the table. She grabbed it and knocked Ms Moon out with it! As Elena was about to leave the room, she saw a piece of paper with everyone's names on and every name was ticked, except for hers…

Elena realised that all of the kids had been captured and she was the only one who was still free, so the teachers must be looking for her. She snuck out and banged another 'teacher' on the head, knocking him out cold. She bolted to the art stairs and ran to the bottom. Weirdly, the fire-escape door was unlocked… She ran out and started yelling for help, then spotted a bike next to the open gate. She jumped on the bike and sped off.

Typical Monday

Ethan Chapman

When your uniform is still dripping with water on Monday
morning
and you realise you have five tests that day
and the adults are telling lies about how they forgot to get you
some money to take to school
and you're watching Bradford lose again and sinking to the
bottom of the league
and you're eating your least favourite food for dinner: chicken
and when you finally go to bed, you walk into a room of mess,
knowing you are going to have to clean all of it up

Five Things Teachers Hate

Paris Dosanjh

1. Kids playing with those little skateboard-things and flinging them across the room.
2. Kids talking over them when they're explaining the work.
3. Kids wandering round the corridors because they don't want to go to lessons.
4. Kids throwing food at each other in the cafeteria when bored.
5. Kids chewing gum and sticking it under the desk.

Bullies

Isaac Woolford

I came out of school skipping, whistling Coldplay. The bullies walked right past me without saying a word! When I got home, my mum said:

'You are old enough to know. You were adopted.'

I gritted my teeth and walked away silently. I made my friends promise to not tell anyone. They were shocked and literally hugged me as soon as I told them. But soon they broke their promise and told everyone in our whole school.

I came out of school roaring like a raging bull. The next thing I knew, the bullies came up to me and one said, 'Imagine being adopted!', then walked away, buzzing.

I said, 'At least my parents chose me. Your mum did not have a choice.'

The bully got mad and charged at me like a rhino.

I went home in a strop. I checked in the mirror: a bruise was coming up. So I said to my mum, 'I am going to start kickboxing!'

Disappeared

Isabelle Stead

I didn't know if I'd done anything wrong but Mum just walked past me and ignored me, so I learned to deal with her neglect. After Mum was out of the picture, it was just me and my dad and my sister. My dad was a sensitive man. He never let me mention Mum. I didn't know where she was or if she even existed. I stopped asking about her when my dad lashed out and asked if I loved my mum more than him. I gave up on having answers. Dad left my sister to do everything herself.

School was hard. No friends, and even the teachers didn't speak to me or help me, so I decided to get home-schooled. I couldn't deal with the stress of having to do work with ignorant people and no help. My dad was a way better teacher. I trusted him but I still felt alone. I wanted to be included and to socialise, but no one talked or acknowledged me. I felt worthless but I knew I had one person and that was enough for me.

One night, my sister was crying in her room. I went to ask her if she was ok, but as usual I got no reply. She walked into my room like I wasn't there. I thought she might finally open up but all she did was bring out a picture of me and some flowers and start praying.

When I heard the words, 'I wish you were here, Jazmine,' I started freaking out. I thought it was a prank or a joke, but she started sobbing.

I was scared and went to my dad to tell him what my sister was doing. I shouted at him to tell me again and again, but he didn't notice. I repeated over and over, 'Tell me! Tell me!'

The Truth About The Lies Your Parents Told You

Various Authors

Santa is a convict, hands cuffed behind his back.
Vegetables are not the best thing to eat.
'Gay' does not only mean 'happy'.
Turning on the light in a car is not illegal.
Watching TV too closely will not make your eyes go square.
The Easter Bunny is a creepy kidnapper who bribes you with chocolate eggs.
Green monsters will not come to eat you if you don't go to sleep on time.
Your heart is actually a potato as cold as ice.
If you step on the cracks, snakes don't snap at your heels.
They are not your family; they are fake replacements.

Jess on the Train

Jemimah Baylis and Emily Noble

Jess just wanted to feel important. But standing outside that huge house made her feel anything but. She took her girlfriend's hand and stepped up to the door.

One day earlier

Jess looked down at her phone. Not one message from her family – it was like they didn't even care. She ignored it and tried to put it out of her head. This trip needed to go well, and she feared it wouldn't. Jess knew that if it didn't, it might change her life.

Stepping onto the train, people gave Jess and Ella funny looks. Annoyed, Jess looked down at her pink knee-high boots. They had seemed like a good idea at the time. They were her confidence boots. Now she regretted them. By now, everyone would be looking for her and her pink knee-high boots. She slumped down into the seat and sighed. It was going to be a long night…

The train jolted and her eyes flew open in shock. It was dark outside the window already. She guessed it must be about 11 p.m. by now. Jess looked over at Ella, who was still asleep, her hair covering her face, and smiled. Her phone buzzed on her leg.

James: Are you ok? You and Ella weren't in school today. J

Jess ignored it.

Twelve minutes and they would be in London. Twelve minutes and they would be in the place that had been on her mind for the past two months. Twelve minutes and they would be in the place that… .

The train stopped with a screech, and they got out of their seats. The doors opened and they stepped off the train onto the platform. It was the biggest station she'd ever seen. The last time she'd been to London was in the car with her mum.

One short walk later, Jess and Ella flopped onto the hotel bed, full of worries about tomorrow. Jess looked down at the floor, guilty that she'd had to steal money from her mum to pay for the train and hotel, but it had been the only way. She'd been so scared. Until Ella reminded her that this time it was her choice and her idea to do this. Last time had not gone well.

Two months earlier: Jess's fifteenth birthday

A man walked into their house. He was tall and looked anxious. Of course, Jess's mother knew exactly who he was: she just didn't tell Jess that this was her dad, finally showing up after fifteen years. Jess was so confused. Up until then, she had believed her mum's husband was her dad. He had gone to Parents' Evening every year when her mum was working. PARENTS' evening. Jess liked him being her dad – he was her dad. Except he wasn't. It was all a lie.

Ella was amazing, though. She was round every day after it happened, being so supportive. And Jess's family all loved Ella. Jess was just disappointed that all that changed when they came out.

Jess's mum and stepdad were always fighting so Jess and Ella liked to hang around at the park twenty minutes from her house. They would spend their time talking or listening to music, or just sitting there, holding hands when no one was around. Jess wondered if her real dad, who lived in London, might be more accepting.

Ping.

Another notification from her friend James. Jess almost wished it was her mum. She was now regretting not telling him her plan, though he had to have guessed by now. She ignored the message and her eyes slowly got heavier and heavier until she fell into a pool of tiredness.

She would need her energy for tomorrow.

*

Ella shook her arm; it was already 11.30 a.m. and she had agreed to meet her dad – Edd – at 1 p.m. She rolled out of bed, dragging herself to the bathroom.

Opening her bag, her black trousers stared longingly at her; she had decided to wear them but now she was second-guessing the idea. What if they were too formal? Maybe she should've worn her flappy dress instead. God, she was nervous.

Once she was dressed she went downstairs, where she saw Ella with a piece of toast in hand, a smile on her face as always.

'You ok?' Ella asked.

Jess nodded, still shocked she was doing this.

It was time to go.

Jess's hands were shaking as they walked to the tube station. It seemed so much further than it had last night.

*

As the tube started to rumble, Jess and Ella sat down in their seats. Jess took a deep breath, reminding herself it would all be ok, no matter what happened. No matter what happened – even if he wanted nothing to do with her – she would have answers.

The tube pulled up at their stop, Jess's nerves flooding her as they stepped off the tube and onto the platform. Jess was still unsure if this was what she wanted. She reminded herself it was, and continued. They had a house to find.

They finally got to the house. It loomed over them: scarily big and extremely daunting. The shadow of the house made Jess shiver as they walked past the perfectly-cut grass.

Jess just wanted to feel important. But standing outside that huge house made her feel anything but.

She took her girlfriend's hand and stepped up to the door.

Her hands were shaking as she knocked.

Mistaken Identity

Jemimah Baylis and Emily Noble

Not-Brenda speed-walks down the street, casually zipping up her dress and eating a sandwich.

Alison: Hey! Hey Brenda, how are you? I've been chasing you down the street for ages!

Not-Brenda: Uh – yeah I'm fine, I guess. Are you trying to sell me something or – ?

Alison: What? No, just wanted to catch up!

Not-Brenda: Huh? I don't think –

Alison: Did I tell you Jacob has gone to university now? Time flies! Don't waste it with your two kids.

Not-Brenda: I don't have –

Alison: How's Charles, by the way? I heard he and my Jacob met up last weekend to talk about him going to Liverpool – does he want to go to Liverpool? It's great by the way. Although I do miss him, you know. David and I think we will change his room into a library. What do you think you'll do when Charles moves out?

Not-Brenda: I'm sorry, I really have to go get my train. I'm late for a date.

Alison: Oh, a date? But I thought – what about Greg?

Not-Brenda: Oh, um, OK. Greg?

Later that day, Alison texts a message to Brenda. It reads:
'Hey, it was great to see you today, I didn't realise you were dating. Did you and Greg break up?'

Alison waits and receives a text back from Brenda. It reads:
'Erm, no. We didn't break up and I did not go on a date! I didn't see you today!?!?'

Alison: Ohhhhh!

Alison walks home, her face bright red.

Steps To Becoming Your Perfect Self

Various Authors

Wake up with an open mind.
Get out of bed on the right side in the morning.
Learn how to play guitar.
Take a walk outside by a river.
Enjoy what you have and who you have.
Get a pet dog.
Play board games and never cheat to win.
Abuse what little power you have.
Listen to music you love.
Keep a journal.
Be a sweet potato.
Get taller.
Get a life.
Do nothing, you are already as perfect as Tom Holland.

TOM HOLLAND
TO DO:

What We Had

Kinza Farah

Humanity is like a scorching flame.
It kills, harms and destroys.
The natural world is dying because of our actions.
Polar bears swim for hours at a time,
nearly freezing to death,
just to find something to appease their appetite.
From the buzzing bees
to the towering sunflowers
to the gentlest of elephants that marches through the deserts
and the blue whales that roam our unforgiving seas,
every part of wildlife is suffering.
The diggers that destroy forests and demolish habitats.
Plastic bottles and shopping bags thrown on the floor.
We think the problems will solve themselves,
but whoever starts it
needs to end it,
and that is us.

Look around,
take a walk, and admire
the elderly oak trees that stand tall
and the families of rabbits and deer.
So if it disappears,
you can remember
what we once had.

Sadness

Paris Dosanjh

If you met it, you'd meet it in the middle of the ocean,
where it's really foggy.
It would have greyish-blue skin: wet and scaly.
watery blue eyes,
messy hair,
bad posture
and gills.
Its fingernails would be sharp
but broken
and it would be
alone.

Calm

Joseph Hopton

Through the gates of dawn, the enormous guru statues towered over the garden. In the middle was Calm, the ruler of the gardens and the keeper of peace. Lilies floated in the crystal-clear waters with koi swimming gently around. The bonsai trees swayed in the wind and the cherry blossoms bloomed.

I walked calmly and slowly towards Calm. The temple towered over everything and you could see it for miles around. On the carpet of the temple, I removed my shoes, bowed and knelt in front of him to begin my prayer:

'Calm please guide me through these dark times and give me courage to proceed with my life. Amen.'

Calm rose and began:

'For a while I will grant you my impregnable oasis. However, I will press you with some rules. One: you must not damage any plant or animal here. Two: you must worship me every day. Three: you must not confess my secrets to the outside world. You may go now.'

I walked away feeling happy, admiring the beauty of the garden until a dark red storm swirled towards me. I turned around and started running away, fear erupting out of my chest. An arm grabbed me and span me around.

A deep, croaky voice said, 'Hello, mortal!'

He said it like it was an irritant, spitting out:

'I am Jealousy, I mean to take over this garden from Calm, but only if you help me!'

I responded quickly with: 'No!' But Jealousy tried to persuade me. He told me, 'Think about it: all of this garden ruled by you and me.'

The thought gave me a shiver down my spine, but it also made me feel purposeful and up for it.

'OK,' I said, 'but we cannot hurt any of the garden.'

Jealousy agreed, but with a sly smile. It made me uneasy, but there was no way to change my mind because, before I knew it, he was within me, and I was walking back to the temple. Calm saw me there and smiled, noticing nothing different in me.

I began with, 'Hello, Calm.' I said this with a growl and a frown on my face.

Oh no, I thought, *Jealousy is controlling me, and I can do nothing about it.*

Calm frowned at the greeting. I continued.

'Give over – you're no ruler. You don't deserve to be here!'

That had really done it, but before anything could happen, Jealousy jumped out of my soul, grabbed Calm, and summoned his minions to chain Calm to the doors of the temple.

'Was there any need to do that so violently?' I asked.

Jealousy laughed.

'Hahahaha – that's only just the beginning!'

He put his hands together and I was blinded for a second by the heat searing my skin. He threw a ball of magma, fire and lava, setting a patch of grass on fire. In no time, the entire garden was on fire. It caught on a willow tree overhanging the pond. The baby koi cowered close to the safety of their parents. I turned again and saw a group of squirrels encircled by fire. Finally came the cherry on top – or more like the fuel on the wildfire – the huge, towering temple crashed down, crushing trees and animals alike.

I cried out, 'Nooooooooooo! You promised me you wouldn't damage the garden!'

Jealousy laughed at that as well, growling, 'Hahahaha – you fool! You actually believed me! Now, my minions, seize him and chain him next to his beloved god!'

He laughed his dreaded evil laugh. Again, I could do nothing, and I didn't want to say anything. All I could think was, *WHAT HAVE I DONE!?*

I had let Jealousy take over.

A Creature Called Courage

Leia Young

On this splendid day, I was walking in the woods when I heard rustling in the trees.
I guessed it was a bird, but I heard no chirping.
I then guessed it was a squirrel, but when I looked up it had no tail.
It was an odd creature: marmalade orange with six long, bandy arms.
I noticed it climbing to the very top of the towering tree.
I could only just hear it mumbling – in English, I thought.
I shouted up to it, 'Get down, it's dangerous!', hoping it would understand.
It leaped down from the top of the tree, frightening me. How did it not hurt its feet?
I looked closely at the creature, not sure where it came from or what it was.
It had the skin of something like a lizard, and its three large green-and-brown eyes
stared at me, straight into my soul.
The creature smelt like the forest: grass, bugs, pond, mud.
It breathed very deeply, I could hear every breath.
As it stared at me, it started to get excited and began to jump around.
Maybe it thought I was a new friend. I could be! It seemed fun.
It grabbed hold of me and dragged me deeper into the forest, running.
All I could see were the trees.
It let go of me and left me on some leaves and I watched as it ran around,

doing crazy jumps which no one should ever do –
doing flips off jagged rocks and fighting big bears.
It could jump off a cliff and easily climb back up.
I felt scared and in shock. I wished it were me, so brave at risk-taking.
It fed off its surroundings, eating bark, berries and leaves.
I could see that every move it made was a risk, but it was having fun.
I left, remembering I could find this creature again at the centre of this dense wood.
I'd made a new friend I would never forget.

Next time I will climb up a tree with this creature
and maybe jump off something too.

Anxiety

Aamna Hussain

I met an unusual creature today.
Its body was shaking like an earthquake.
Its breath was rattling and shallow.
Sweat rained down its face.
Its fingernails were bloody.
Its lips were a half-eaten strawberry.
Its voice was like nails being scraped on a chalkboard.
You will meet it too, in a time of struggle,
So be prepared.

ABCDEFGHIJ
R

Perplexity

Eleanor Anness

Perplexity creeps inside you when least wanted, with no right to be there.
It will show when you get asked an important question
With an answer that doesn't come easily,
Like, 'What is life?'
Or, 'Did you know that this boy likes you?'
Its existence chills you to the bone.
The spikes down its back puncture your skin with each touch.
Its snake-like tongue wraps itself around your neck.
It slowly sucks the air out of your lungs,
turning you into a soulless shadow
so all words leave your mind at the most important moment.
Your brain becomes like a mushy piece of cake.
This menace is called perplexity.

Dissociation

Jemimah Baylis

I met a creature once. It was there but not there: a mere shadow crawling across the floor. I asked it if it wanted a friend, but it was too distracted to listen. It could not understand what I was saying. After a while, it started to run away from me, like it was too scared to admit that it could see me. Distressed, it sat there rocking on the ground. It was not communicating anymore, and I didn't think it ever would again.

I met a creature once. It was there but not there.

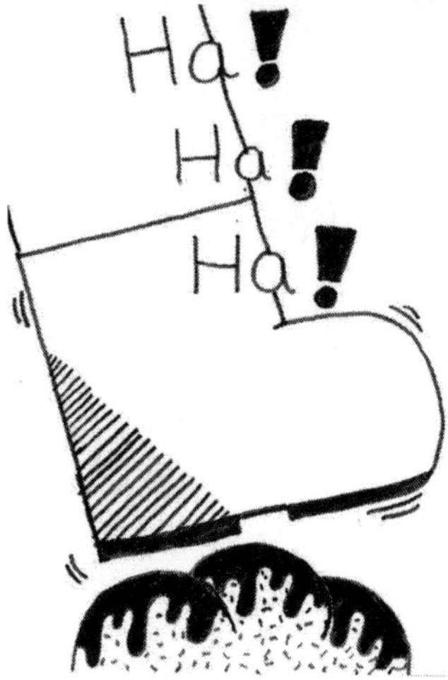

Karma

Isaac Woolford

Don't you hate it when… ?

You take credit for someone else's IQ
test and their name is the same as
yours and you come last.

You laugh at someone else's ice cream falling, and then you
slip on it.

You bring a speaker to school to look cool but then you realise
it's been called off because of a strike day.

You take your friend's drink from them and down it, then wet
yourself in front of that friend.

You steal a Snickers bar from a child and it triggers
your allergies.

You make fun of someone's skill level
in a game of football, then in a
couple years' time they start a
career at your favourite club.

You read steps on how to get a
girlfriend and do everything it
says, then the last step says,
'Keep dreaming.'

Ten Ways To Ha-Ha About Pain

Dexter Yorke

1. Shout 'I'm dying,' when you have a tiny cut.
2. Start making sprinkler noises when you start bleeding.
3. Pretend to pass out when you are hit on the head.
4. Speak in a funny accent.
5. Overact by screaming and rolling around on the floor.
6. Make weird noises.
7. Fake-cry as though you've been shot.
8. Breathe in loudly.
9. Hit someone else.
10. Become a dinosaur.

The Sad Businessman

Kinza Farah

The businessman scowled at the car in front's brake lights as he realised he was already late for his first meeting. To distract himself he chose to play the song, 'Walking on Sunshine', which put him in a good mood. Suddenly his internet connection crashed, so he had to resort to playing the radio. A song came on that his mum had loved before she passed away. Tears started to fall, and he hung his head. He walked slowly into the meeting, his hands shaking and his body trembling. During the meeting he couldn't get his brain to focus, as he sat staring into space, thinking about the song. His boss, who was leading the meeting, asked him about the project, and he decided to stand up and take a break outside. He slid down the wall and onto the floor with his head in his hands. After the meeting finished, the song sprung back into his head, reminding him of how he and his mum would dance to it. He heel-clicked and pranced back to his car, humming the song on repeat.

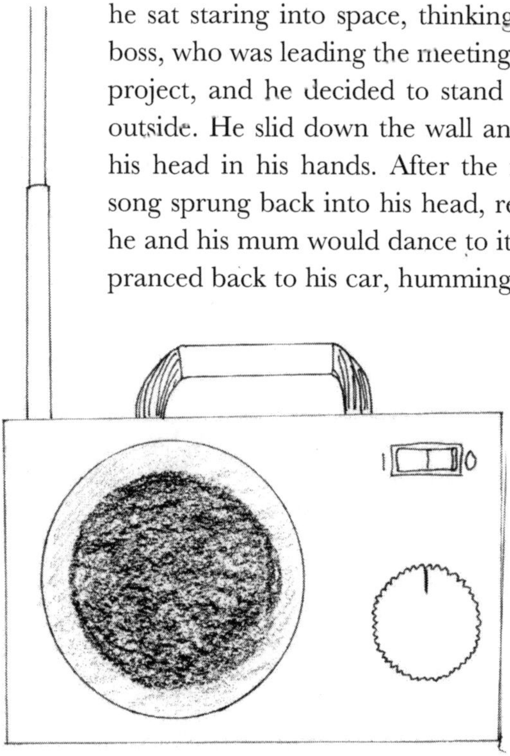

If Everything Went Backwards

Various Authors

We'd be born at one hundred years old
And our hair would retract inside our scalps.
We would go from old to young,
waking up at sunset,
starting school at 3 p.m.,
finishing at 8.45 a.m.

We'd give birth to our mothers and fathers.
We'd turn nocturnal.

Dogs would walk humans around the park
And we'd walk on our hands,
Which would be our feet, and be hairier than our heads.
Australian spiders would be tiny and British ones massive.
We'd wear ice skates on concrete.
Murder would be legal, along with all other crimes.
Potatoes would eat humans with salt and vinegar.

Water would be as dry as the desert.
The Earth would be the sun.

PARK
SNEY'S latest animated ad

Goldfish

Neve Curtis

Lying still on the floor of the tank, I feel a twitch in my tail. A shiver runs through my scales as I begin to flap about. My gills start to work again and a sudden rush of blood refreshes my body. I'm alive! I jump up and down, watching the water float upward towards my empty tank, seep through the hole in my home and flood around me. A feeling of joy! The cat seals the hole with her claw, with a devious look on her face. She slowly backward-walks away and I am free to roam my tank.

How To Blow Out Your Candles (Backwards)

Jemimah Baylis

The flame ignites and I suck in the air.
The embarrassment leaves my body, like a crowd dispersing, as
my friends and family inhale the words of 'Happy Birthday'.
I shake the match down and up to re-light it.
I lower the match back to the wick and scoop the flame onto it.
I strike the match up the packet and the fire goes out.

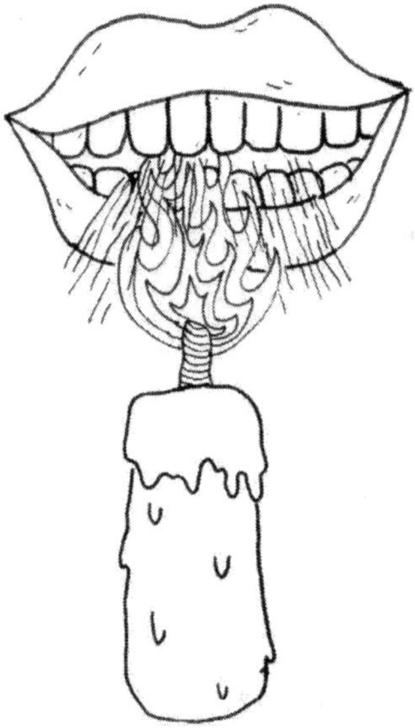

How To Be More Potato

Various Authors

Dig a hole and sleep in it.
Chop your head, legs and arms off.
Dig yourself out of the hole you're buried in.
Plant yourself to grow more friends.
Run away when they try to cut you up like a silly sausage
(we will live forever).
Drink water when it rains.
Be small.
Bathe in soil.
Sit in an oven, then get slit open and covered in cheese
and tuna.
Have only potato friends.
Get fried and covered in salt and flavouring.
Be chips. Be crisp like tree bark.
Be gnocchi.
Be roastie.
Be mash.
Be jacket.
Be croquette.
Be new.
Be baby.
Be you.

Ten Steps To Getting A Girlfriend

Hector Sheehy

1. Grab a pillow.
2. Grab a blanket.
3. Be cool by scoring from the halfway line.
4. Tell hilarious jokes or squirt milk out of your nose.
5. Have curly hair like Harry Styles.
6. Be amazing by doing a flip-reset-double-tap.
7. Don't be a bozo like a Messi fan.
8. Be like me.
9. Joking – be you.
10. Keep dreaming.

Myths

Joseph Hopton

Throwing salt over your shoulder is good luck.
The ancient Greeks thought that people were made of clay.
Heaven.
Four-leaf clovers mean luck.
Egyptian blood is made of gold.
It's impossible to breathe through your nose with your tongue
    stuck out.
Bigfoot.
If you can't touch your toes, you're cleverer than someone
    who can.
Hell.
We only use ten per cent of our brain capacity.
Ronaldo is better than Messi.
Only five per cent of people can complete Einstein's riddles.
Water is able to cool lava from a volcano.
Bees die when they sting you.
Wasps can tell each other apart from the patterns on their
    abdomens.
Dua Lipa is better than Ariana Grande.

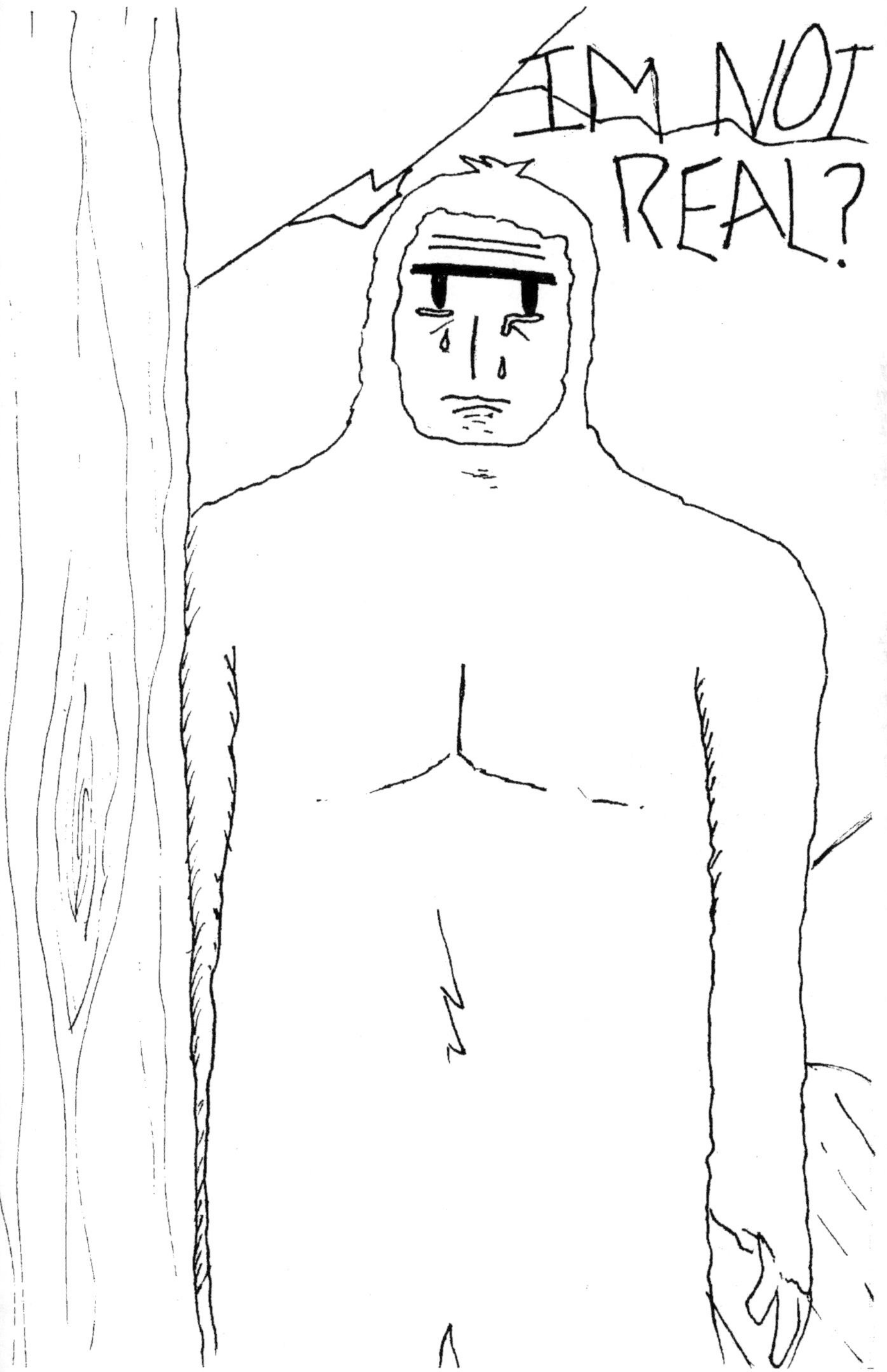
IM NOT
REAL?

Fire

Neve Curtis

Feels hot and rough to touch.
Roars and crackles like a witch with a bad cough.
Gobbles up human after human,
becoming fiercer and angrier with each life it takes.
Has a mesmerising warmth deep in its heart
and pulls me in like a cosy hug,
as though it might protect me from the dangers of the world.
Then turns and attacks me,
pushing me away like a bad smell.
Maybe he is the danger
I am just not seeing,
on the other side
of the wall he's creating.

The Executioner

Eleanor Anness

The royal executioner's dream was to stop all public executions. But the king had made it so that anyone who protested against the death penalty would be punished by execution. The executioner was sick of the cracking sound of the spine as the axe went through their necks.

His solution was to commit treason: he would kill the king and pray that the new monarchy would feel the same as the executioner. He spent a week studying how the guards operated around the castle, before killing one of them and stealing his uniform. But the executioner was not a familiar face to the other ten guards, so he stabbed the other ten guards in the chest.

The executioner got into the room where the king slept but then chickened out. He spent the next week full of regret and guilt over not killing the king. He went on a walk along a cliff and wanted to jump off. When he got to a section with no fence, he felt like it was the perfect time to jump, but someone tapped him on the shoulder.

He turned around to see the princess. She told him that things would never change. He went home sad and questioning life, and was arrested by the police for the murder of eleven royal guards. He spent the rest of his life in prison and lived sadly ever after.

Mother Time

Estelle Outlaw-Bentley

Entry One: Abandoned Church (Place 31)

12 p.m.

I start to wonder about the haunted estate.

2 p.m.

I did not really believe, but… nothing can deny it. No, NOTHING in this world is worse than this. Nothing…

4.30 p.m.

A trailing fog twists and winds around the deserted perimeter of the silent graveyard. The gravestones are being reclaimed by Mother Time. The trees are shaped like giants bearing down upon the world we know as Earth.

The whistling wind grows louder and louder. Sweat drips down my head. But why? It's not even hot. Goosebumps litter my arms, but not from cold.

An unearthly scream fills the isolated area. I can hear my heartbeat pulsing. The last remaining light drains from my face.

6 p.m.

What is that? What thing could make that sound?

The trees seem to swallow me up and spit me out over and over again.

A ghastly un-human soul approaches. It looks deprived of life: dressed in a torn black gown, its eyes scooped out like ice cream. My body fizzes as the thing limps closer and closer and closer.

I snap out of my trance and start sprinting towards a rickety shed.

BANG!

I slide down against the ramshackle door. My eyes widen, my pupils dilate, and I start to tear up.

Then I see it.

A small body.... blood drained from it... only a kid... wearing a pink dress.

It would be the height of a bear cub, if it were stood on the ground, but it hangs from the roof like a chandelier.

I take some shallow breaths and try to think logically.

As I try to figure out a way to escape, I see movement from the dead child. The mouth twitches, then all I see is blood.

Sleeping Chaos

Various Authors (led by Milly)

Their brain impersonated independence
so my heart was sleeping chaos.

Their hands laughed fear
when my veins jumped anger.

Their eyes were munching disappointment
but my eyes were sprinting loneliness.

Their head killed flamboyance,
yet my arms tumbled happiness.

List of Uncomfortable Things

Lewis Ward

Wearing a jumper you can't take off.
Water spraying everywhere when you wash your hands.
Someone spitting on you when they're talking.
When you pick up a cookie and it crumbles in half.
Wearing shoes that are too tight.
Forgetting your toast is still in the toaster after ten minutes.
Getting your new clothes dirty.
When you ask for no toppings on a burger, but you get them
anyway.

All These Brilliant Things

Various Authors

When your crush looks at you.
Swimming in an outside pool while it's raining.
The smell of fresh bread.
Not getting water on your jumper when you wash your hands.
Watching butter melt.
Tea and toast.
Someone dancing in slow motion.
Peeling glue off your hand.
Seeing a police officer eating a doughnut.
Your raindrop winning in the race on the car window.
Your cat sleeping on your pillow. Falling asleep to her purrs.
YouTube.
Listening to music so loud you cannot hear anything else around you.
Watching a TV show over and over again.
Crying while watching sad Bollywood movies with your Mum.
Uncreased book covers.
When a car goes through a puddle and soaks you at the side of the road.
Shepherd's pie.
Arriving at a concert and realising the wait is over.
When you drop your lanyard in a drain and a cat thinks it's a toy, then follows you all the way home.
New pens.
Letting yourself cry when someone cheers you up.
Laughing so much you can't breathe, and keeping adding things that make it funnier.
Surprise trips to the cinema.

Y

Watching a kid's ice cream fall on the floor.
You and your friend getting picked to be partners in PE.
Boys-versus-girls dodgeball.
Chlorine.
Watching someone's face when their biscuit falls into their tea.
Birdsong.
Squirting a fresh bottle of whipped cream straight from the fridge into your mouth.
Peculiar olde-worlde pens.
Being cosy in a blanket when there's snow outside.
Scaring your brother and sister when they least expect it.
Hyperfixating on a show.
Getting exactly what you want for your birthday.
Getting to skip school because you were sick twenty minutes after breakfast.
Scoring a last-minute goal in a cup final against a team of players from your school, so you get bragging rights.
Ritz crackers with cheese.

Fluffy socks.
Home-made knitted scarves.
The plastic cover from your new phone screen.
The smell of old comic books.
The Victory Royale sound in *Fortnite*.
The crunch of leaves.
Watching clouds pass.
Birthday-cake icing done perfectly.
Seeing fresh cereal in the cupboard.
Steam coming off your hot chocolate in cold weather.
Fire.
Kids falling over.
Holding a baby and they fall asleep.
Silence.

Biographies

Eleanor Anness: Drawing weird things, listening to music and taking photos – that's all you need to know about me.

Charlie Babbitt: Hello. Hi. :)

Arthur Barrett: www.youtube.com/watch?v=dQw4w9WgXcQ

Jemimah Baylis: If I were a food I would be kiwi fruit. If I were a time of year I'd be the start of September. If I were an animal I'd be a bee. If I were a drink I would be Sprite. I am a trip on a long-distance train.

Eve Butcher: What can I say? I'm a gorgeous, talented, amazing individual.

Cailum Castillo: I'm organised, responsible and… umm… I like tacos.

Ethan Chapman: I love football and my favourite snacks are Haribos

Sage Craig:
I was alive yesterday.
I'm alive today (I think).
But I might not be alive tomorrow.
So I'll live every day like it's my last.
Really stressed out.

Neve Curtis : Hi, I'm Neve – chatty and energetic!

PARIS DOSANJH: I am a fighter jet with missiles; a victory dance after winning. I am not a deadly disease. I am a black-and-purple electric guitar. I am The Swarm at Thorpe Park. I am New York cheesecake. I am burnt pizza. I am a moody gremlin.

TIA-ROSE ELLINGTON: I consider myself to be very creative and have a passion for arts and crafts. I love watching tennis and football with my family and I also love to bake. Friends and family are really important to me. In my free time I read, paint and watch Netflix. I am writing this in Year Nine, just after my fourteenth birthday, and who would have thought I would be published in a book at this age?

KINZA FARAH: I am a mountain bike rocketing down a steep hill. I am spicy chicken drumsticks paired with curly fries. A shining sunset after a long, tiring day of writing. A neon-pink electric guitar blasting music. The white rabbit from Alice in Wonderland, who is always in such a rush. The beautiful country of Tunisia when the sun has hit its peak in the sky. A high-diver doing tricks off the five-metre platform. The best sister, daughter, friend, lover and person in the world.

MIA GODEK: Smart, pretty, caring, kind, confident and musically gifted – or so my friends say.

JOSEPH HOPTON:
I am a lightning storm. A Ferrari F1 car. A deer with lots of stamina.
I am Mr Bump from the Mr Men. I'm a charity donation.
I am a mountain bike. A really tricky question on the hardest test.
I am a chest-pumping, angry-shouting, boastful idiot.
I am a precious sapphire mixed into the jungles of the Amazon.

AAMNA HUSSAIN:

Name:	Aamna Hussain
Likes:	burgers, baking, beauty
Dislikes:	chips, Tuesdays, some animals
Ambition:	to become a therapist
Superpower:	shapeshifting

ARABELLA LEWIS: I don't really know what to write so I'm just going to give you some advice from @prestonpalmo that really struck something in me when I read it:

'Life doesn't give you the people you want. It gives you the people you need – to help you, to hurt you, to love you, to leave you and to help you grow into the person you are meant to be.'

STANLEY MARTIN:
Likes: video games, films, art, design tech, friends, business, computer science, money, staying up really late on weekends.

LIAM NATHAN MCNICHOLAS: Creative, kind, yellow.

PAEGAN MOON: I was born on 15th June 2009. I am now fourteen and I'm now in a published book. I have two brothers and two half-sisters. I have a pet hamster (Elvis) and a pet dog (Raffy).

JACK NICHOLSON: I am him.

Emily Noble:
I'm a highland cow on a breezy mountain.
A 10p lolly from the corner shop.
I'm a bullet train rattling through the station.
A red grape shining in its punnet.
I'm a half-empty (or is it half-full?) Tango can.
I'm a pinky-purple sort of colour.
I'm an autumn wind in summer.
I don't really make any sense.
I'm Emily.

Bryan Norminton:
I'm very artistic
Very kind to others who are kind
Only patient from time to time
And very nutters

Estelle Outlaw-Bentley: Unpredictable, loud and very proud to have been runner-up in the First Story Six Word Story Competition.

Julia Robb:
Finishing a book
Finishing a climb
When you draw something perfect first time
The peacefulness of a bookshop
Heavy rain and a storm
And freshly-baked cookies that are warm
I like music
Pasta is the best food
Starting a good book puts me in a good mood

HECTOR SHEEHY:
I am a 200cc Honda dirt bike.
I am Bart Simpson.
I am Ritz crackers.
I am a monkey climbing a tree.
I am 36°C sunny weather.

ISABELLE STEAD:

Nickname:	Izzy
Age:	fourteen
Favourite food:	noodles
Things I like:	art, animals, writing
Things I dislike:	spiders, tomatoes
Favourite drink:	juice
Favourite colour:	green

CHARLIE TURNER:
I get lost.
I meet friends.
I get home.

LEWIS WARD: I'm thirteen, I like to play football and my favourite footballer is Erling Haaland.

BRANDON WILLIAMS:

Age:	fourteen
Nickname:	Bdog
Likes:	sports cars, RC cars, football, Fast & Furious
Dislikes:	mushrooms, the colour pink, dolls, rain, horses

Most commonly-asked question: 'How tall are you?'
Dream sports car: Lamborghini Urus

Isaac Wilson:
I am Isaac, a boy who loves sport.
I am a boy who likes to play.
I am a boy who is weird, funny and a lot of things.
I am me.

Isaac Woolford:
I share with my friends 'cause I care.
I like my steak medium rare .
I can play good passes.
I never skip classes.
I'm in love with my curly hair.

Dexter Yorke: I am a boy who likes music, animation, nerdy stuff, video games, animals and hanging out with my friends. I am a meteor heading towards a distant planet.

Leia Young: I am a mature cheddar-cheese sandwich. I am a small brown pug that loves its family. I am Belle when she saves her dad. I am a cloudy blue sky at midday. I am peach iced tea and a grand piano playing pop-rock. I am thirteen. I am an auntie, a sister, a friend and a daughter. I am a dog-owner, a dancer, an art lover. I am Leia.

Acknowledgements

Katie McLean for typesetting this anthology.

Kirsten Irving for copy-editing and Sarah Donnelly for proofreading this anthology.

Jenny Dack for designing the cover of this anthology.

Foysal Ali at Aquatint for printing this anthology at a discounted rate.

The Founders of First Story:
Katie Waldegrave MBE and William Fiennes.

The Trustees of First Story:
Ed Baden-Powell (chair), Carey Scott (treasurer), Aziz Bawany, Hannah Brown, Sue Horner, Sarah Marshall, Bobby Nayyar and Ella White.

First Story Ambassadors:
Patrice Lawrence MBE and Tracy Chevalier FRSL.

Thanks to our funders:
Jane & Peter Aitken, Amazon Literary Partnership, Authors' Licensing & Collecting Society, Arts Council England, Blue Thread, Fiona Byrd, Charlotte Aitken Trust, Drapers' Charitable Fund, Garfield Weston Foundation, Goldsmiths' Company Charity, John Lyon's Charity, John R Murray Charitable Trust, Julia and Hans Rausing Trust, Man Charitable Trust, Mercers' Company Charity, Paul Hamlyn Foundation, teamArchie, Wellington Management UK Foundation, the Friends of First Story and our regular supporters, individual donors, community fundraisers and those supporters who choose to remain anonymous.

Pro bono supporters and delivery partners including:
Arvon Foundation, BBC Teach, British Library, Cambridge University, Centre for Literacy in Primary Education, English and Media Centre, Forward Arts Foundation, Goldsmiths, University of London, Hachette, Manchester Metropolitan University, National Literacy Trust, Manchester and Nottingham UNESCO Cities of Literature, Nottingham Trent University, Penguin Random House, Rathbones Folio Prize, University of Greenwich, University of Huddersfield, University of Hull, University of Leicester, University of Manchester and University of Nottingham.

Most importantly, we would like to thank the students, teachers and writers who have worked so hard to make First Story a success this year, as well as the many individuals and organisations (including those we may have omitted to name) who have generously given their time, support and advice.